Phonics Storybook

The Blue Brook

Written by **Mariam Seedat** and **Francis Ulrich**

CARAMEL TREE

Bruce is a blue fish.
He lives in a blue brook.

3

Brenda is a blackbird.
She sits on a broken branch.

Brenda looks into the brook.

She sees the blue fish.

Brenda brings a blueberry.
She drops it in the brook.

The blueberry floats.
Bruce wants the blueberry.

Brenda wants Bruce.
Watch out, Bruce.

Bruce blows bubbles.

Bloop. Bloop. Bloop.

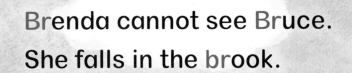

Brenda cannot see Bruce.
She falls in the brook.

Brrrrr.

The brook is cold.

Bruce has the blueberry.
Brenda sits on the broken branch.

Let's Sing!

Bruce, Bruce is swimming.
Brenda is sitting.
They both want to eat. (x2)

He is a blue fish.
She is a blackbird.
They both want to eat. (x2)

Drop down a blueberry, (x2)
Into the brook.
It is so cold.

He swims to get it.
She goes to get him.
Bruce blows some bubbles. (x2)

Drop down a blueberry, (x2)
Into the brook.
It is so cold.

Bruce, Bruce is okay.
Brenda is all wet.
She fell in the brook. (x2)

Drop down a blueberry, (x2)
Into the brook.
It is so cold.

blue

brook

black

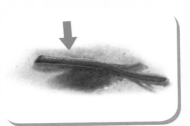

broken

branch

blueberry

drop

float

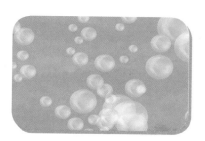

bubble

sit

fall

cold

Consonant Clusters

☐ Look and learn.

| bl | br |

blue

black

brook

blueberry

blow

branch

Look and write.

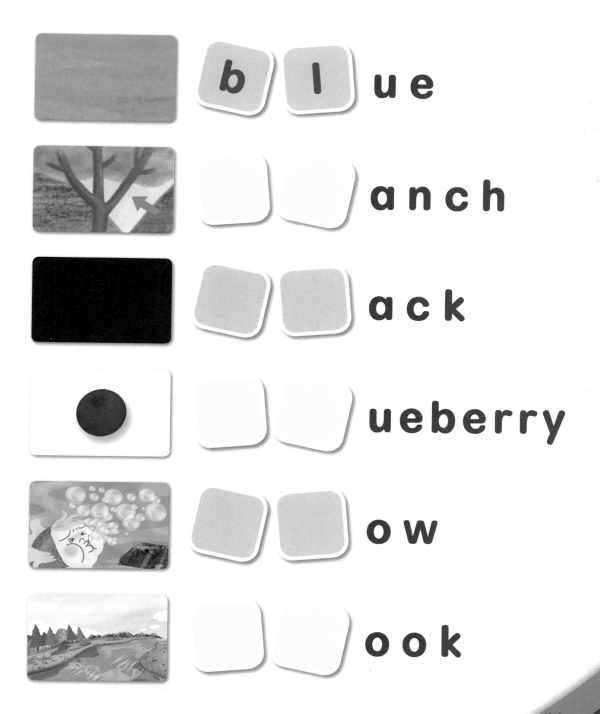

b l u e

___ ___ a n c h

___ ___ a c k

___ ___ u e b e r r y

___ ___ o w

___ ___ o o k